Fip's
Magical World
of Color

Written & Illustrated by
Susan Carlson Scott

New Concord Press™

Fip's Magical World of Color

Written & Illustrated by
Susan Carlson Scott

First Edition

ISBN 1-887932-94-1
Library of Congress Control Number 2002111942

Printed in U.S.A.

New Concord Press is a division of Equine Graphics™ Publishing
P. O. Box 8016, Zanesville, Ohio 43702-8016
http://www.newconcordpress.com

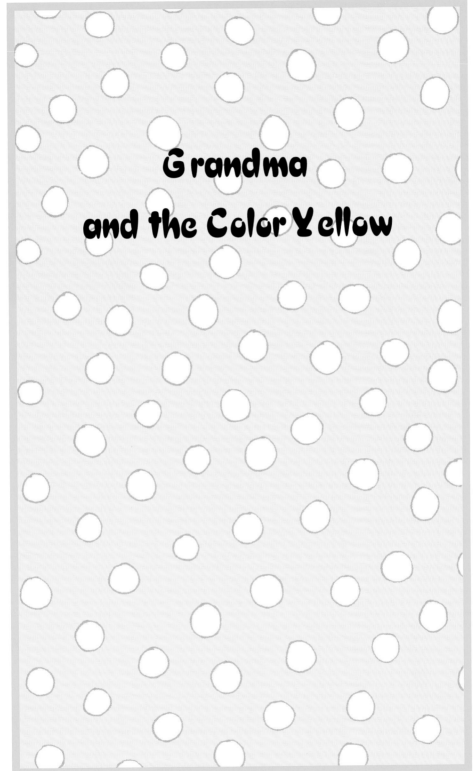

Grandma
and the Color Yellow

Early on Saturday morning, Margaret heard her Grandma's voice coming from downstairs. She quickly dressed and ran down to see her.

"Grandma!" cried Margaret.

"Hello, dear!" Grandma said, as she gave Margaret a big hug and a kiss.

Grandma had on her usual Saturday outfit: her yellow dress with the white polka dots and a yellow bonnet.

"Are you ready for our walk?" Grandma said with a wink.

"I sure am," Margaret said happily.

Margaret loved her Saturday walks with Grandma. She looked forward to them all week long.

Grandma held Margaret's hand and off they went toward the meadow behind Margaret's house.

As they reached the edge of the meadow, Margaret could smell all the wonderful flowers.

Margaret was growing more excited the closer they got to the center of the meadow.

Soon, they reached the clearing where a park bench stood all alone. Grandma and Margaret sat down on the bench. Grandma took her bonnet off and placed it on the grass beside her.

"Are you ready?" she asked, smiling.

"Yes!" cried Margaret cheerfully.

Margaret remembered back to the first walk through the meadow with Grandma. It was then that Grandma had shared her secret with Margaret.

Grandma had a magical power, a power over the color yellow. She could do whatever she pleased with it. She could make the sun shine a brighter shade of yellow, change a white rose to a yellow one, or even change the color of Margaret's hair ribbon from purple to yellow.

But there was a special trick that Margaret enjoyed the most, and as she thought about it, Grandma was already starting her magic.

"Look at this," Grandma said to Margaret, as she pointed to a red tulip growing near the bench.

"Watch now," Grandma said as she waved her hand over the flower.

When she drew her hand away, the red tulip was no longer red. It was orange!

"Hurray!" cried Margaret. "That's great, Grandma!"

"What does this mean?" asked Grandma.

"Yellow and red make orange!" shouted Margaret.

"Yes," said Grandma happily. "Okay," she whispered, "Let's try another one."

She turned and picked a blueberry from the bush
behind the bench.

"Here we go," she said.

Grandma waved her hand over the blueberry.

"Green!" Margaret shouted and clapped her hands. "Yellow and blue make green." She clapped again.

Grandma grew quiet and sat very still for a moment.

"What's the matter Grandma?" said Margaret, a little worried.

"Oh, nothing, dear," replied Grandma, smiling. "Say, let's try something new, Margaret!"

"Okay," said Margaret, not sure what the new trick would be.

Grandma pulled a red scarf from her pocket and placed it in Margaret's hand.

"Now close your eyes," she said.

Margaret closed her eyes and waited for Grandma to perform her magic. Grandma held Margaret's other hand in hers.

"Concentrate on the color yellow, Margaret," she said.

"Okay," said Margaret.

As she concentrated, Grandma moved Margaret's hand across the scarf.

"Open your eyes," she said gleefully.

Margaret opened her eyes and looked down at the new orange scarf.

"Great trick, Grandma! cried Margaret. "Do another one!"

"I can't," said Grandma.

"What?" said Margaret, puzzled. "Why can't you do another trick?

"You see, dear," said Grandma, "I don't have the power anymore."

"Your power is gone?" said Margaret sadly. "Where did it go?"

"To you, child," said Grandma as she held Margaret's chin.

"I don't understand, Grandma," said Margaret.

Grandma said, "I know someone who can explain it to you better than I can."

Then Grandma called out, "Fip!"

A swirl of smoke surrounded Grandma's feet and suddenly a tiny woman was standing before them.

"Hello, Fip," said Grandma.

"Hello, old friend," said Fip, smiling.

Fip placed her tiny hand on Margaret's shoe and said, "Well, you must be Margaret."

"How do you know my name?" asked Margaret, quite bewildered.

"Your Grandma has told me everything about you," said Fip, happily.

"I don't understand," said Margaret, still puzzled.

Fip answered, "Let me explain."

"You see, every fifty years I give the power of a color to a child. Fifty years ago, when your Grandma was ten years old, I gave her the power of yellow. Her fifty years has now passed and she asked that her special power be given to you. Is this power something you would like to have?"

"Oh, yes!" said Margaret. "I have always loved yellow and the tricks that Grandma could do with it."

"All right," said Fip. "But let me warn you, your power over yellow is to be used only for good things and only to bring pleasure to others. It is your job to show others the beauty of this color. Your Grandma tells me that she trusts you to do this.

"Can I trust you, Margaret?" said Fip sternly.

"You can trust me, Fip," replied Margaret.

With that, Fip disappeared in a puff of smoke. Margaret turned to her Grandma and gave her a big hug.

"Thank you, Grandma," she said.

"I love you, Margaret," said Grandma. "I want you to know the happiness and pleasure I have received from the power of yellow."

"Are you sad that you no longer have the power?" asked Margaret.

"Oh, no, dear," she said with a smile. "I am so happy that I could give it to you."

"Shall we go home?" asked Grandma.

"Yes," said Margaret. "Grandma, next Saturday, I'll do magic just for you!"

Grandma smiled and laughed. She hugged Margaret tightly as they headed for home.

Simon
The Blue Whale

Simon was a beautiful blue whale.

Simon loved the sea and all the creatures that lived near his home.

One day while Simon was out for his daily swim, he felt the water around him moving in a strange way.

Simon remembered a rule that his father had once told him about what to do when the ocean moved strangely.

His father had told him to dive deep down into the sea to protect himself!

Just as he dove, he was missed by a large net that brushed over his body and passed by his huge tail.

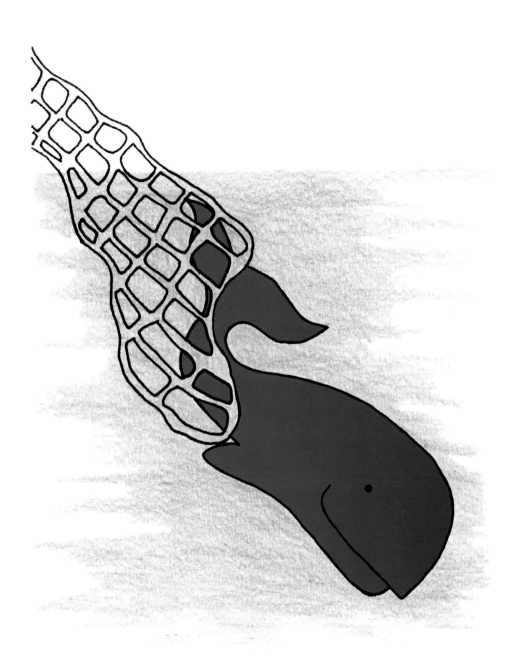

Simon dove deeper, then turned to look up from his hiding place behind some rocks.

He could see many of his friends and other sea creatures.

They were trapped in a net and being pulled to the surface!

Simon was very sad for his friends.

Simon did not know exactly where they would be taken, but he was sure it was not somewhere pleasant.

When the movement in the water stopped, Simon felt safe enough to return home.

When he arrived back home, he told his parents what had happened.

"Simon," said his father. "You were lucky today. Tomorrow you may not swim in that part of the ocean."

This made Simon very unhappy. He loved that part of the ocean. There were so many beautiful fish there and his friends always played there, too.

The next morning, Simon decided not to listen to his father, and he left home for his usual daily swim.

The ocean was cool so Simon decided to swim closer to the surface. He wanted to warm himself in the sun.

Simon had only been on the surface of the water for a few minutes when that terrible movement of the water started again.

Simon dived and started to swim towards the bottom of the ocean. He felt the rough ropes of a net surround his body.

He tried to swim away, but the net tightened and began to pull him to the surface.

Simon was very scared. Then he suddenly remembered what his mother had told him. If he was ever in trouble, he should call out a magical name.

"Fip!" cried Simon. "Fip, please help me!"

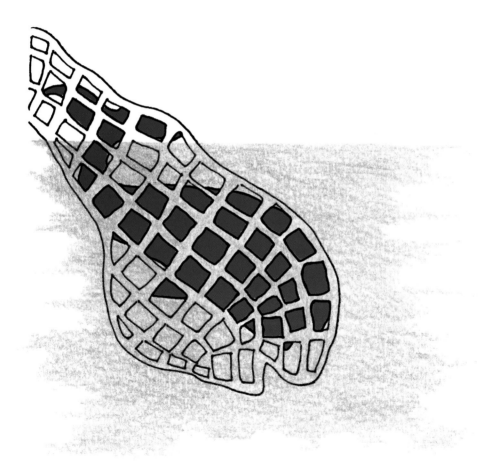

Simon was still being lifted up to the surface of the water when a tiny woman appeared from nowhere.

"Are you Fip?" asked Simon.

"Yes," said Fip. "You called me and here I am. It looks as if you have gotten yourself into some trouble."

Simon said, "Yes, I was not supposed to play here today, but I did not listen. The nets are going to take me away! Can you help me?"

Fip said, "I will help you, but you must promise not to swim or play here ever again."

Simon nodded. "I promise."

Fip reached into her bag and pulled out two wands. One was red and one was yellow.

She touched Simon with the wands and a wonderfully strange thing began to happen.

Wherever she touched Simon with the red wand, he was turning purple. Wherever she touched him with the yellow wand, he was turning green.

Simon could not believe his eyes!

The net had finally pulled Simon to the surface and he was hanging several feet above the water.

Simon could hear shouting from the boat.

"Look at that!" one man yelled.

"What is it?" another man said.

Yet another man said, "Cut it loose. He is some kind of strange fish, not the whale we are looking for."

Simon could feel the rope begin to loosen and suddenly he was free!

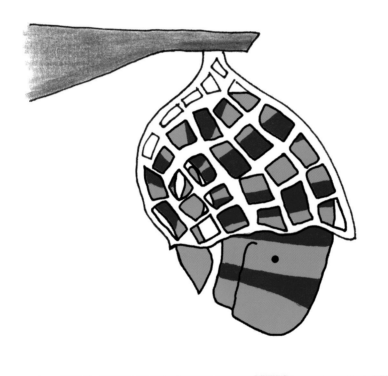

As he began to dive deep down into the water, his skin began to change from green and purple back to the color blue.

As he was leaving the forbidden play area, he turned to thank Fip. She had disappeared!

He whispered "Thank you," smiled, and swam toward home.

Alex
and
the Color Red

Alex rose in the morning feeling very happy and excited. Today is very special.

Today is Alex's birthday.

All week long he had been hoping for a certain surprise that he had wanted for a very long time.

Alex rushed downstairs, still in his pajamas.

He could hear his parents talking in the kitchen. They had been up early making Alex's favorite breakfast: blueberry pancakes.

His parents smiled as Alex ran into the kitchen.

"Happy Birthday, Alex!" they exclaimed. "How is our big boy this morning?"

"I'm fine!" shouted Alex, happily.

Alex turned toward the kitchen table. His face lit up with glee to see the table decorated in honor of his birthday.

Before him was a banner that said "Happy Birthday," three polka-dotted party hats, and presents all around his plate.

This was all wonderful, but as soon as Alex saw the great big box in the corner, he jumped up and down. His parents laughed.

"Go ahead and open it, Alex," said his dad.

Alex rushed to the box. The surprise he had wished for was finally here.

He ripped the pretty paper away from the box as fast as he could. He clapped with happiness as the paper fell away.

There it was! A bicycle!

His dad helped him open the end of the box. Alex shook with excitement. He put his hands inside the box, grabbed hold of the cold handlebars and started to pull.

He could see the shiny silver spokes coming toward him. He gave a hard tug and the bike bumped out onto the kitchen floor.

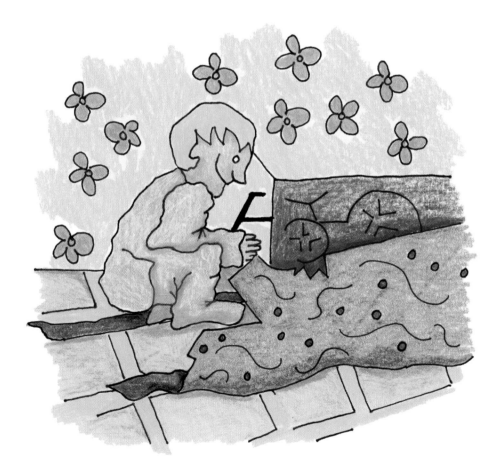

Alex's smile disappeared. He looked up at his parents and began to cry.

"I wanted a purple bike, not a red one!"

Alex ran from the kitchen and into his room. His parents could hear him shouting, "Not a red one! Not a red one!"

Alex lay on his bed clutching his favorite stuffed animal. It was a purple puppy dog. His name was Rex. Alex loved Rex as much as he loved purple.

"I don't like that dumb old red bike," Alex told Rex. "I wish there was no such thing as red!"

"Hey, you! Little Boy!" A tiny voice was shouting.

Alex was startled and looked up to the place where the voice was coming from. He was surprised to see a little woman about the size of his thumb. She was standing on his bed post.

"Who are you?" asked Alex.

"My name is Fip," shouted the tiny voice.

"Where did you come from?" asked Alex.

"I come from the Land of Colors! I hear that you have a problem with red," she snarled.

"Yes, I do," said Alex. "I don't like red. I wish there was no such color!"

All of a sudden, Fip twirled and disappeared in a cloud of white smoke.

Alex blinked his eyes.

"Where did she go?" he cried.

Alex looked down at Rex and shrieked at what he saw.

His favorite stuffed animal, which was his favorite color purple, had turned blue!

"Rex! What's happened to you?" shouted Alex.

Alex heard a noise coming from around his room. It sounded like a popping noise that was growing louder and louder.

He looked around the room. His eyes grew wider and wider. His room was changing!

Everything that had been orange was turning yellow! And everything that had been purple was turning blue!

"How could this be happening?" said Alex. "It must be that little woman. She must have done this!"

"Fip!" shouted Alex. "Fip, you come back here right now!"

A swirl of white smoke was starting to appear on the bed post. Little by little, a small figure began to form.

"You called?" said Fip, with a tiny smile on her lips.

"I want to know what you did to my colors!" demanded Alex.

"Well, whatever do you mean?" said Fip, smiling shyly.

"You know, you know!" snapped Alex. "My orange and my purple!"

"Oh, yes, yes," she said, tapping her finger to her cheek. "Your orange and your purple have gone back to the Land of Colors. They cannot live here anymore."

"What do you mean?" said Alex. "Why can't they live here?"

"They had to leave," said Fip. "They had to leave to be with red."

"Red?" cried Alex. "What does red have to do with this?"

"You see," said Fip, "Orange and purple need red. Red helps them. Without red, orange and purple cannot be."

"I don't understand," said Alex. "Why did Rex turn blue and my orange balloon turn yellow?"

"It is simple," said Fip. "When red and blue live together, they make purple. When red and yellow live together, they make orange."

"You sent red away," said Fip, sadly. "So yellow and blue have to live alone now."

"I don't want them to be alone, Fip. Do you think red could come back to live with me?" asked Alex, shyly.

"I do not know," said Fip. "You said some awfully mean things about him."

"I'm sorry," said Alex. "I really want red to come back!"

Fip winked. "Okay. This is what you have to do."

She looked at Alex for a moment and then pulled a bright red ball from her pocket.

"You must take this ball and throw it into the air," she said, placing the tiny ball into Alex's hand.

Alex threw the ball into the air. Fip began spinning very fast. The ball silently exploded in the air.

Soft round drops of red were falling from where the ball had been. The droplets began touching everything that used to be orange or purple.

Alex watched with excitement.

Soon, everything was back to its original color.

Alex smiled and shouted, "I *love* red!"

He looked down at the bed post, but Fip was gone.

Alex smiled and whispered, "Thank you, Fip."

Alex knew what he had to do. He jumped from bed carrying Rex with him. He bounded down the stairs and into the kitchen.

His parents were standing next to the bike looking very sad.

"I'm sorry, Mom and Dad," said Alex. "I love you and I love red!"

Smiling, he said, "This bike is the best bike in the whole world!"

The Day That Black Ran Away

Fip stretched out on a big fluffy cloud. She was tired.

She had spent another long day painting the skies and meadows.

Her eyelids were just about to close when she heard shouting coming from below.

Someone was calling her name.

Fip rolled closer to the edge of the cloud so that she could hear what the voice was saying.

She peered through the cloud and saw Orange jumping up and down screaming, "Fip! Fip! You must come down!"

Fip grabbed her bag of colors and floated down to where Orange was standing.

"What's wrong?" she asked.

Orange cried, "It's Black! He's run off!"

Fip was puzzled by this. No one had ever wanted to leave the Land of Colors before.

"What do you mean, he's run off?" she asked.

"I don't know," said Orange. "He was crying and saying something about not belonging here."

"What?" shouted Fip. "Of course he belongs here! Tell me which way he went."

Orange pointed down the road which led to the edge of the forest.

Fip hurried off, hoping that Black had not gotten too far.

Fip searched for a long time. She could not find him behind the rocks or the trees.

Fip was worried. It would be night soon and she had not yet painted the sunset.

She was just about to give up when she heard weeping coming from a clump of bushes.

She cleared the way and found Black sitting on an old fallen tree stump.

"Black," said Fip, "Are you all right?"

Black turned to her and began to cry even harder.

"Please leave me alone, Fip," sobbed Black.

"I want to help you," said Fip. "Tell me what's wrong."

"I don't belong to anyone," said Black, still crying.

"What do you mean?" asked Fip.

"I don't have any family," sniffled Black.

"We are all your family," said Fip softly.

"No!" shouted Black. "I've been made from no one."

"I don't understand," said Fip.

Black wiped his eyes and sighed.

"Orange was made from Yellow and Red.
Purple was made from Red and Blue.
Green was made from Blue and Yellow
and I was made from no one!"

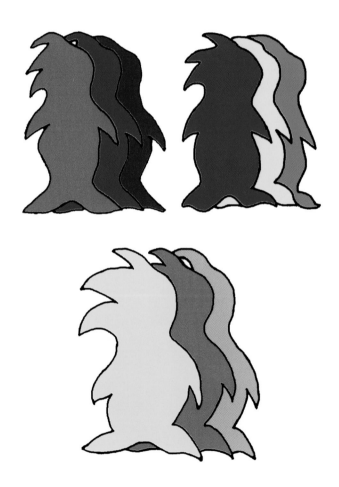

"That's not true," said Fip, smiling gently. "If you will come back to the Land of Colors with me, I'll show you something that will make you happy again."

Black rose from the tree stump and followed Fip out of the forest.

Fip led him to the middle of town.

"Wait right here," she told him.

Black watched her as she floated to a nearby roof top. As she landed, she took a deep breath and began to speak.

"All those who belong to the Land of Colors, please come to me at once!"

Her voice rang out over all of the roof tops, from one side of the town to the other.

Doors and windows could be heard opening throughout the town. They all began to gather together.

It was a beautiful sight to see all of the colors. They were all so friendly.

Black smiled for a moment and then grew very sad once again.

Fip floated down next to Black. The town grew quiet. She turned to Black and smiled warmly.

"I want to show you that you do belong with us," she said.

"We love and care about you very much. Why, if it wasn't for you, the stars would never be able to come out at night. They need your darkness to hold them.

"Without you, children would not have shadows to follow and protect them.

"Beautiful music could never be played. It needs the notes that you make."

"Now," she said, "I want you to watch very closely."

Black was curious. Fip pulled one Yellow, one Blue, one Green, one Purple, one Red, and one Orange from the crowd. She lined them up in a row.

Gently, she put her arms around all of them and, with one giant squeeze, she tightly hugged them together.

Black could not believe his eyes!

As she pulled them into one another, they became one brand new, beautiful color! Fip carefully took her arms from around the new color.

She looked at Black and said, "See! You are made from all of the colors, which makes you very special. Everyone here is part of your family."

Black looked at the new color that was just like him. He smiled brightly. The new Black smiled back.

Black shyly said, "Fip, thank you for helping me. I really do have a family. A great big one!"

Everyone laughed and cheered. Fip looked toward the sky.

"It's getting awfully late! I'll have to hurry if I'm ever going to get the sunset painted," she said.

"How would you and your new friend like to come with me? You can hold my bag of colors for me.

"When we are finished, we'll see if we can make some of those stars shine!"

The three of them held hands and floated high into the sky.

All was well once again in the Land of Colors.